D0045306

Hi, I'm JIMMY!
Like me, you probably noticed the world is run by adults.
But ask yourself: Who would do the best job
of making books that *kids* will love?
Yeah. **Kids!**

So that's how the idea of JIMMY books came to life.
We want every JIMMY book to be so good
that when you're finished, you'll say,
"PLEASE GIVE ME ANOTHER BOOK!"

Give this one a try and see if you agree.
(If not, you're probably an adult!)

JIMMY Patterson Books for Young Readers

JAMES PATTERSON PRESENTS

Sci-Fi Junior High by John Martin and Scott Seegert

Sci-Fi Junior High: Crash Landing by John Martin and Scott Seegert

How to Be a Supervillain by Michael Fry

How to Be a Supervillain: Born to Be Good by Michael Fry

How to Be a Supervillain: Bad Guys Finish First by Michael Fry

The Unflushables by Ron Bates

Ernestine, Catastrophe Queen by Merrill Wyatt

Scouts by Shannon Greenland

No More Monsters Under Your Bed! by Jordan Chouteau

There Was an Old Woman Who Lived in a Book by Jomike Tejido

The Ugly Doodles by Valeria Wicker

Sweet Child O' Mine by Guns N' Roses

The Family that Cooks Together by Anna and Madeline Zakarian, daughters of Geoffrey Zakarian

The Day the Kids Took Over by Sam Apple

THE MIDDLE SCHOOL SERIES BY JAMES PATTERSON

Middle School, The Worst Years of My Life

Middle School: Get Me Out of Here!

Middle School: Big Fat Liar

Middle School: How I Survived Bullies, Broccoli, and Snake Hill

Middle School: Ultimate Showdown

Middle School: Save Rafe!

Middle School: Just My Rotten Luck

Middle School: Dog's Best Friend

Middle School: Escape to Australia

Middle School: From Hero to Zero

Middle School: Born to Rock

Middle School: Master of Disaster

Middle School: Field Trip Fiasco

THE I FUNNY SERIES BY JAMES PATTERSON

I Funny

I Even Funnier

I Totally Funniest

I Funny TV

I Funny: School of Laughs

The Nerdiest, Wimpiest, Dorkiest I Funny Ever

Word of Mouse
Give Please a Chance
Give Thank You a Try
Big Words for Little Geniuses
Bigger Words for Little Geniuses
Cuddly Critters for Little Geniuses
The Candies Save Christmas

For exclusives, trailers, and other information,
visit jimmypatterson.org.

Patterson, James, 1947-
Dog diaries. Curse of
the mystery mutt /
2020.
33305248403838
mi   11/03/20

...OL STORY

DOG DIARIES

CURSE OF THE MYSTERY MUTT

JAMES PATTERSON

WITH STEVEN BUTLER

ILLUSTRATED BY RICHARD WATSON

JIMMY Patterson Books

Little, Brown and Company

New York   Boston   London

The characters and events in this book are fictitious. Any similarity to real persons, living or dead, is coincidental and not intended by the author.

Copyright © 2020 by James Patterson

Hachette Book Group supports the right to free expression and the value of copyright. The purpose of copyright is to encourage writers and artists to produce the creative works that enrich our culture.

The scanning, uploading, and distribution of this book without permission is a theft of the author's intellectual property. If you would like permission to use material from the book (other than for review purposes), please contact permissions@hbgusa.com. Thank you for your support of the author's rights.

JIMMY Patterson Books / Little, Brown and Company
Hachette Book Group
1290 Avenue of the Americas, New York, NY 10104
jimmypatterson.org

First North American edition: November 2020

Originally published in Great Britain by Penguin Random House UK, October 2019

JIMMY Patterson Books is an imprint of Little, Brown and Company, a division of Hachette Book Group, Inc. The Little, Brown name and logo are trademarks of Hachette Book Group, Inc. The JIMMY Patterson Books® name and logo are trademarks of JBP Business, LLC.

The publisher is not responsible for websites (or their content) that are not owned by the publisher.

The Hachette Speakers Bureau provides a wide range of authors for speaking events. To find out more, go to hachettespeakersbureau. com or call (866) 376-6591.

ISBN: 978-0-316-43007-4

Cataloging-in-Publication data is available at the Library of Congress

10 9 8 7 6 5 4 3 2 1

LSC-H

Printed in the United States of America

For Griffin and Haru
– S.B.

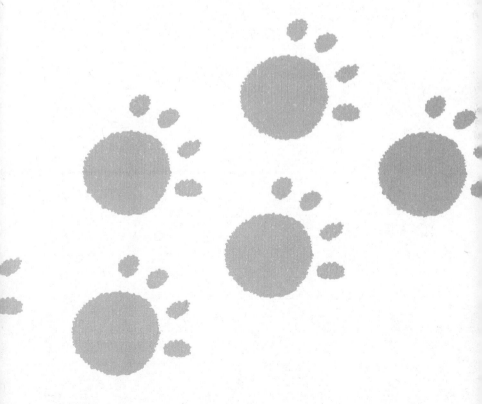

AAAAAAAAAAGH!

Something terrible is going on, my person-pal! Something so dreadful, it's enough to curl your tail with terror (if you had one, of course) or turn a Dalmatian's spots white with fear.

I...I...I can't figure it out! Just last week, everything was fine and dandy. I was a contented canine, going about my SNIFF-A-RIFFIC days in a happy haze of doggy treats and tummy rubs. But now...

Run, my furless friend! Go hide!

Anywhere! It doesn't matter...in the laundry pile outside the Rainy Poop Room...

under the Food Room table...

behind the garbage cans in the backyard! GO, GO, GO! Take this book with you and find somewhere snuggly and secret, before you turn the page.

Okay…are you safely tucked away? Have you made sure there are no snooping snouts or nosy neighbors listening in? Good!

What I'm about to tell you will make your toes shiver with shock! Brace yourselves.…

Ready?

Okay…

THERE'S A MYSTERY MISCHIEF-MAKER ON THE LOOSE IN HILLS VILLAGE!!!

Wait a second…you're supposed to be more shocked than that, my person-pal. Didn't you understand what I said?

Oh…I know what you're thinking. You're reading this, scratching your human head and wondering what on earth I'm talking about, right?

Well, I haven't told you all the details yet. You won't believe what's been happening, my furless friend. It's awful! A disaster of pooch-apocalypse proportions! It's…

STOP EVERYTHING!! What am I doing? In all my shock and panic, I completely forgot to introduce myself.

If you've read any of my books before… HI! IT'S GREAT TO SMELL YOU AGAIN…but if this is the first time you've ever opened one of my LICK-A-LICIOUS diaries, you'll have no idea who I am, and that's a TERRIBLE way to start a good story.

Well, there's only one way to fix that...a proper introduction.

Don't worry, I'm not about to sniff your butt, my person-pal. That's how us pooches usually do it, but, just for you, we'll do it the Peoplish way.

My name is Junior Catch-A-Doggy-Bone. HELLO!

And I live with my pet human and his person-pack in

Junior
Catch-A-Doggy-Bone

the snuggly-buggliest kennel in the whole of Hills Village. Well…I think it is, anyway, and I'm practically a genius, so I'm certain to be right.

Here they are.…

~~RAFE~~ Ruff ~~MOM~~ Mom-Lady ~~GEORGIA~~ Jawjaw

~~THE KHATCHADORIAN FAMILY~~
The Catch-A-Doggy-Bone Pack

Ruff is the GREATEST pet human a mangy mutt like me could ask for, and I love him with all my houndy heart. Just the thought of him coming home from school at the end of a long day makes me want to yip-yap and happy-dance for hours, let me tell you!

Ever since Mom-Lady brought me back from the Hills Village Dog Shelter—or as I like to call it...POOCH PRISON!!!—my life has been one great big bundle of BARK-TASTIC BLISS.

Well, it had been until things started going bump in the night...I'd say that's enough of an introduction for now. It's about time we got back to the fur-raising story.

Ummm...where was I? Oh, yeah...

It was only three days ago that this vile villain first struck our town, and things haven't been the same since. I'll explain....

Last Friday

9:47 a.m.

I had just arrived at the dog park, pulling Mom-Lady on my leash, and I could already sense that something wasn't right. I'd barely slept the night before, my person-pal, and if there's one thing I'm really, really, REALLY good at, it's sleeping…and eating…but MOSTLY sleeping!

You see, something had kept me awake... something horrifying, and I'm not talking about my archest of enemies who lives in the hallway closet—THE VACUUM CLEANER...

Nope! It was far worse...

I'm talking about an eerie howling in the night that jangled my bones and prickled my whiskers with fear. It was a high-pitched, whiney yowl and it echoed through the streets like something from one of the scary moving pictures I've watched with Ruff on the picture box.

Now, normally I love watching those things...

I do love them, honest I do! I only pretend to be afraid so Ruff doesn't feel...y'know... embarrassed when he gets scared. But I gotta admit to you, my person-pal, the howling that night was far scarier than any mutant monsters or vampire villains.

Anyway...

After I'd reached the dog park with Mom-Lady, peed on the gate and crossed the playing field, I spotted my mutt-mates huddled near the jungle gym and I knew...I just knew they'd heard the horrible howling too, and were every bit as spooked as I was.

MY PETRIFIED POOCH-PALS!

It didn't take long before we were all waggy-tongued and yapping about last night's strange events.

DID YOU HEAR IT?!
I THINK IT WAS THE GHOST OF MY UNCLE FWUFFY!
IT MADE MY TAIL TREMBLE!
HUH?
I COULDN'T EAT MY KIBBLE!
YIKES!

The only one of us who didn't hear a thing was Genghis...

He's normally the most nervous of the pack, but, lucky for him, he missed all of it.

You see, the little guy picked up a pretty impressive case of fleas from his neighbor's cat, Doris, recently...

IMPRESSIVE INFESTATION

The Hills Village veterinarian put Genghis on some MEGA-STRENGTH new flea medication that makes him super-snoozy and he slept right through the howling! I feel kinda jealous!

But...

Not all of us were so fortunate, my furless friend. This is the part that gets scream-aliciously terrifying! Brace yourself...

Just as we were yapping away, sharing our versions of the strange events...Lola burst into tears. She was a complete muddle of whimpers and whines, I swear! At first we couldn't get anything out of her except sobs and a few worried woofs, until finally she said...

I think those words will haunt me for the rest of my life, my person-pal. Have you EVER heard anything so awful...so unspeakable... SO CLAW-CURLINGLY PETRIFYING?!?!

Oh, wait…I'm forgetting that you, my fur-less friend, are a human…and to a person like you, that probably doesn't sound quite so dreadful. Let me explain…

If you've never had the pleasure of having your life poochified by a masterful mutt like me, you may not know how IM-PAW-TANT it is for every dog to have their favorite toy. I'M BEING SERIOUS! Our days would be mean-ingless without them. It makes no difference how big or small or pampered or mangy or scary or growly or fluffy or dirty or scratchy or jumpy or yappy or happy or grouchy you are…it is one of the oldest rules in the licky-law books that every pooch must have a best-best-BESTEST toy to love and chew and play with when their pet humans aren't around.

Now, that all might sound a little puppy-ish to you, my person-pal, but it's true. A mutt's life is not worth living without the joys of a great toy to cherish.

Every pooch on the planet has one, but we're all very different and have our own personal tastes when it comes to picking our favorites.

For example…my tip-top-treasured-trinket is my STICKIEST STICK!

OH BOY! I LOVE THAT THING SOOOOOOOOO MUCH! It makes my tail go crazy just thinking about it.

I found my perfect stick last fall when Mrs. Haggerty, the human-lady across the street, was piling up a great big bundle of tree bits to make a bonfire in her front yard. I smelled its STICK-A-RIFFIC goodness the second we'd left our front door, and I managed to yank on my leash and drag Ruff over there just in time to rescue this YUM-A-LUMP-TIOUS wonder from being sizzled on the sidewalk.

My stick lives in pride-of-place under the bed in Ruff's Sleep Room and I only take it out for a chew on the most special of occasions.

My mutt-mates all have their best toys too.

Odin carries a special slipper with him everywhere around his kennel…

Diego is practically in LOVE with Squeaky
Penguin…

Genghis has
his tug-a-licious
rope toy…

Betty is head-
over-paws for her Roly-Poly-Peanut-Butter-
Squirtin'-Ball…

And then there's Lola...My houndy heart could break just thinking about her sad little face.

I left Mr. Fuzz-Butt out in the backyard before I went to sleep... you guys know it's most fun to chew him when he's all squidgesome and mildewy the next morning... but when I woke up... HE WAS GONE!

It's okay, my person-pal. I know you're probably sobbing like a terrier with a toothache right now...Go ahead, I understand. I think I might have a little sniffle myself...

You see, even way back in the days when my pooch-pack and I were all behind bars in the Hills Village Dog Shelter, Lola had Mr. Fuzz-Butt. She loved that old bear from the tip of his snorty-snout, down to his fuzzy butt.

He was a great toy. One of the best...

It was right at that moment, my furless friend—right then, as Lola was sniffling away—I knew that something horrifying had wandered into our town and we were all in for a SERIOUSLY scary adventure.

DIRT PATCHES
AND STAINS
FOR EXTRA FLAVOR

ONE LEG
LONGER THAN
THE OTHER...
PERFECT FOR
SWINGING

TUBBY
TUM-TUM
FOR SNOOZING
ON

Mr.
Fuzz-Butt

Odin had just suggested we go for a sniff in Lola's backyard to see if there were any clues to be found. We were making plans for how to start the investigation when Betty suddenly yelled...

Everyone gasped in shock as our memories raced back to the months we all spent in pooch prison. In those miserable old days, when we were cooped up for what seemed like an eternity, without so much as a nose boop or tummy rub, we'd while away the hours listening to the stories of a scraggly old chow chow in the cell next to ours. Her name was Old Mama Mange and she'd led the most dog-a-licious life I'd ever heard of. Every night she'd tell us tales about her adventures…

And sometimes, on really rare occasions, she'd tell us everything she knew about you humans, and believe me...she knew a lot!

Of all the human stuff, I loved hearing about your weird traditions and celebrations...especially the Night of the HOWLY WIENER!

On one dark night of the year a **GIANT** howling Wiener sausage visits the town and the street is filled with monsters. They knock on every kennel door in search of treats and all the humans think it's **GREAT!** Humans have cat-hairballs for brains...

I didn't totally believe Old Mama Mange's tales of the Howly Wiener. I mean, who ever heard anything so crazy...or delicious...as a ginormous howling sausage running around town?! But what Betty told us on that morning left my fur prickling. Could Old Mama Mange have been telling the truth? Are we being terrorized by a tasty tube of processed meat?!

Last night, before the howling even started, I heard my pet humans saying the Night of Howly Wiener is next Thursday! It looks as though he's arrived early...

I'd love to tell you what happened next, my person-pal, but I...well...I...

FAINTED!!!

Monday

8:37 a.m.

Okay, my person-pal, I hope that wasn't too spine-jangling for you to read. I guess you probably threw this book across the room or buried it someplace, screaming "I CAN'T TAKE ANOTHER WORD! IT'S JUST TOO HORRIBLE!"

I totally understand, though, my furless friend. This is all HORRIFYING! I swear, I didn't know what to do with myself for the rest of the afternoon after Mr. Fuzz-Butt went missing. I couldn't sleep, I couldn't eat...more than two bowls of lunch and dinner...I couldn't even bring myself to bark at the mailman when he came to the front door with a package after lunch!

My head was swirling with unanswered questions, like...

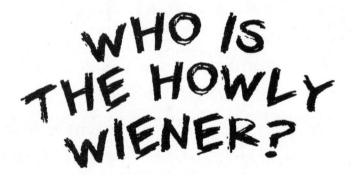

WHO IS THE HOWLY WIENER?

IS IT MADE FROM PORK OR TURKEY?

WHY IS IT HERE?

WHEN CAN I EAT IT?

Do you suppose I need to make a few plans for when I get to meet the Howly Wiener? Hmmmm? Oh, well, it can't hurt, I guess. Licky-law 2789 states that A POOCH SHOULD ALWAYS BE PREPARED! I'll have a think…

HOWLY WIENER PLANS

1. WOLF DOWN THE HOWLY WIENER THE MINUTE I SEE IT.

2. EAT SOME OF THE HOWLY WIENER AND BURY THE REST IN THE BACKYARD FOR LATER.

3. TAKE THE HOWLY WIENER TO THE FRONT DOOR AND HOWL AT THE MAILMAN TOGETHER.

4. SHARE THE HOWLY WIENER WITH MY PARK-PALS.

But, getting back to the story…After our meeting in the dog park on Friday, Odin and Diego scooted straight over to Lola's kennel and had a proper sniff about. No one (except me—HA!) can out-snuffle Odin and Diego… their noses are smell-o-matic masterpieces.

It didn't take long for Odin to find a lit-tle clump of Mr. Fuzz-Butt's extra-fluffy and extra-flavorsome stuffing in the long grass... and that wasn't all! There was also a new smell! When the Howly Wiener stole Mr. Fuzz-Butt, it took a pee and re-scented the exact spot where Lola takes her morning breaks...if you know what I mean.

What is going on, my person-pal?! Can sausages pee?! Us dogs love to mark our favorite spots by peeing on them, but do scary giant sausages do that too? There's something very fishy about this Howly Wiener...

AND! Sure as Meaty-Giblet-Jumble-Chum is the scrummiest food around, the howling has continued every night since. It's getting louder and yowlier and scarier...and with only three more days to go until the Night of the Howly Wiener itself, I'm feeling more nervous than I think I've ever felt. Gulp!

9:23 a.m.

I can't lie, my person-pal. When Betty told us about the Howly Wiener, I had secretly hoped she'd got it all wrong or was just being silly. You know how much she loves to tell jokes. I've had my fair share of WEIRD experiences around the Peoplish Howliday season and I'm not sure I can cope with any more of it.

You humans can be so ODD at times. What with Fangs Giving and Crisp-Mouth, I felt pretty certain there couldn't possibly be anything more confusing in the calendar, but I was wrong!

We've just headed out on our morning trip to the dog park and...and...all my worst fears are coming true!

44

Ruff and Jawjaw are at school, and Mom-Lady needed to visit the grocery store, so before stopping off for a game of fetch and a snuffle around the jungle gym, we went first to the shops on the far side of town.

Normally I LOVE visiting the grocery store with Mom-Lady. I worked out ages ago that if I'm a GOOD BOY (I LOVE THOSE TWO WORDS!) and I wait calmly and patiently outside on the sidewalk while she does her shopping, Mom-Lady will buy me a cheesy or meaty treat from the whiff-a-licious deli counter. So...I'm always a happy hound to go along.

BUT TODAY!!!!

I...I...I don't know what's happened, my furless friend. I barely recognized the store just now...even when we were practically right outside! Instead of being filled with snacks and yum-a-lumptious foods, the front window was stuffed full of spider-webs and spine-jangling monsters!

Now, my understanding of the Peoplish language can be a little crummy at times... but I could definitely read the words across the top of the window. There was no mistaking it. It said "HAPPY HOWLY WIENER"!

HAPPY HOWLY WIENER?!?! What's so happy about it? Why would the humans of Hills Village want to celebrate a night when monsters prowl the streets demanding treats?!?! This is all SO confusing!

9:48 a.m.

AAAAAAAAAAGH! It gets worse! MUCH WORSE!!
　　Mom-Lady finished her grocery shopping

(and forgot to buy me my cheesy-meaty snack, I might add...) and then we headed to the dog park, BUT...outside every building and kennel we walked past there were people complaining that their trash cans had been toppled in the night. Piles of garbage were strewn across the lawns and all the mailboxes had been scratched or chewed.

I think it's safe to say the Howly Wiener has struck again! That terrible trouble-maker is a criminal mastermind, for sure!

10:10 a.m.

The dog park is not the happy place it usually is, my furless friend. It seems more treasured toys have been disappearing and every pooch in town is terrified that they'll be next!

This is worse than I feared, my person-pal...

10:55 a.m.

Once we'd snuffled around the dog park, Mom-Lady took the route home via the Dandy-Dog store, and...

THIS IS A NIGHTMARE!! The whole world has gone bonkers!

Picture this, my person-pal. There we were...me leading Mom-Lady on the leash when we heard the most claw-curling barking and whining coming through the entrance doors.

If you've never visited the Dandy-Dog store before, you won't know that it's a dog-a-licious wonderland and one of my favorite happy-spots in the whole town! It's a POOCH

PARADISE! IT'S A HOUNDY HAVEN! Whenever a dog goes inside that place, they come out grinning from ear to ear and they're the merriest mutt you could imagine for the rest of the day. SO...WHAT WAS THAT AWFUL NOISE COMING FROM INSIDE?!

Suddenly Genghis's pet human walked out of the store with a...a....I leapt behind Mom-Lady's legs in shock!

To my horror, Genghis was nowhere to be seen, and in his place at the end of the leash was some kind of MUTANT SPIDER!!!

11:01 a.m.

Okay...I may have got a little carried away. **WELL, WHO COULD BLAME ME?** Never in my wildest imagination did I expect to see my poor little friend coming out of the Dandy-Dog store dressed like something from another planet!!!

It turns out Genghis and his pet human had been out buying special outfits for this weird-WEIRD-WEIRDEST of celebrations. What is it with you humans and wanting to dress up your pooch-pals all the time? Just last year when it was Crisp-Mouth and the mysterious Saint Lick was coming to visit, Mom-Lady made me wear all sorts of stupid clothes, but I'd NEVER seen anything like this.

Then, before I could even make a run for it, Mom-Lady said...

Oh, don't you look adorable, Genghis! We should get you something to wear, Junior, it'll be fun!

Fun?! FUUUUNNNN?!?! In no time Mom-Lady had dragged me into the Dandy-Dog store without so much as a "GOOD BOY!" and, once again, I found myself being dressed up in all sorts of crazy canine clothing. It was like Crisp-Mouth Eve all over again! Look away if you're squeamish, my furless friend. What you're about to see will make you run and hide under the nearest laundry pile for at least a week.

TURN THE PAGE IF YOU DARE!

12:17 a.m.

Hello? Is that really you, my person-pal? I can't believe you're here and still reading my DOG DIARY after the unbelievable horrors you've just witnessed. But...you'll be glad to hear Mom-Lady didn't buy me an outfit in the end. Haha!

I AM A GENIUS!

After hearing how much my buddy Genghis was whining and barking about his spider makeover, I knew I had to cause even more of a fuss if I was going to escape with my pooch pride.

Every time Mom-Lady and the store

owner dressed me in a new outfit, I wailed
and scratched and flopped all over the floor
until...

Ha! Well, that's one piece of good news, my person-pal. No one outsmarts Junior and gets away with it! I learned the old FLOP AND WAIL trick back when I first came to live in the Catch-A-Doggy-Bone kennel and Mom-Lady insisted I go out into the back-yard even when it was raining.

I don't know about you, but I hate-HATE-HAAATTTEEE the rain. It makes my fur all clumpy and washes out the slobber-licious taste of my last meal from my beardy bristles.

So...the flop and wail has gotten me out of many a close shave, and now I don't have to spend the Night of the Howly Wiener looking like a canine clown! Phewy!

Tuesday

11:00 a.m.

Stop everything, my furless friend. It looks like the Howly Wiener is up to his tricks again!

Mom-Lady and I are just walking past Belly Burstin' Burgers after our morning stroll around the dog park and there's a big crowd of humans outside and lots of police people have arrived in their flashing moving people-boxes on wheels.

Ugh! I can't see through the crowd...

11:01 a.m.

Ha! I knew I could count on Mom-Lady to want to know what's going on. She's nosier than a basset hound sniffing squirrels.

We're heading close for a good look...

11:13 a.m.

Yikes! There's mayhem everywhere, my person-pal. I pulled Mom-Lady to the front of the squabbling people and...and...It's so horrifying I'm not sure I can even get the words out...

Come on, Junior!
   Breathe in…
   Breathe out…
   Breathe in…
   Breathe out…

Okay, I can do this.

Well…Just as I got through the crowd I was hit by the delicious waft of beef burgers and cheese and French fries, and for a moment I thought they must be handing out free samples. Ruff would have been so upset if they had…Belly Burstin' Burgers is his favorite food-spot in the whole of Hills Village.

His snack of choice is a Triple-Cheesy-Nacho-Nosher Burger. It's as big as my head and he LOVES 'em!

Anyway...It was just then I spotted the police people talking to Mr. Moreno (the owner of Belly Burstin' Burgers, who occasionally gives us a treat if my pooch-pack and I wait outside the kitchen door long enough). This is the horrifying part...The poor guy looked completely devastated...just like Lola had!

11:21 a.m.

After hearing Mr. Moreno talking about the snaffled snacks, I knew I had to get inside that place and have a look around. After all, I'm a master of mystery-solving with my sniff-a-licious nose. Maybe the Howly Wiener would still be inside?

Agh! I just thought of something, my furless friend! What if this burger-eating howling sausage was made from beef? That would mean it was a...a...CANNIBAL! I have to catch this monster and end its reign of mischief!

11:22 p.m.

Oh, I'm going to be in so much trouble with Mom-Lady when we get home, my person-pal, but I just couldn't help myself.

Before she could grab tight and stop me, I yanked the leash out of Mom-Lady's hands, ducked under the police people, bolted through the doors of Belly Burstin' Burgers, and...

IT WAS CARNAGE!!

I knew I only had a few seconds, so I instantly sprang into clue-finding mode and scanned the scene for evidence.

You wouldn't believe what I spotted...

For a second I thought I was going to fall down as my mutt-mind started swimming with a squillion questions. PAW PRINTS? HAIRS ALL OVER THE FLOOR?

All this time I've been completely wrong, my person-pal. The Howly Wiener isn't a delicious swindling sausage! It's a...it's a... DOG!!!!

I...I can't believe it. We're being TERRIER-ized by a criminal canine!

Agh, I can barely think straight! What kind of EVIL MUTT-MASTERMIND would do all these terrible things? Think, Junior, think...

It must be some kind of law-breaking Labrador, or wicked whippet! No...it's worse than that. MUCH WORSE! We're dealing with a...a...a MONSTROUS MASTIFF, or an ABOMINABLE AKITA! Maybe even a DEMONIC DANDIE DINMONT!!!

I'm baffled, my furless friend. At least a huge howling sausage would have been pretty easy to find, but there are hundreds of dogs living in Hills Village. It could be anyone! How am I going to stop the poop-etrator now? This is hopeless!

At that moment, Mom-Lady caught up with me and grabbed the end of my leash.

As we headed back outside, I was just about to howl in despair, when I spotted a line of mustardy/ketchupy paw prints heading through the door and down the street. HA!

I can't believe I thought I'd failed. It looks like the Howly Wiener is no match for ME! With my amazing nose—I'm practically a waft-sniffing-whizz—I'd be able to track the smell-trail left by those sauce-covered steps, and they'll lead me straight to the canine criminal!

Hmmmm...I think I smell a plan coming on...

1:57 p.m.

Check…check…this is Special Agent Junior back in action.

Okay, my person-pal, right now, we're back at the Catch-A-Doggy-Bone kennel, but I need to be really quick if I'm going to follow that line of saucy steps and discover who the MYSTERY MUTT is.

Mom-Lady has put me out in the backyard while she's gone to do a shift at the diner. Grandmoo is in the house, but she's snoozing. This gives me three hours before the big yellow moving people-box on wheels drops Ruff and Jawjaw home from school at four o'clock.

In that time I'll have to sneak under the loose fence panel, scamper over to the other side of town, unmask the Howly Wiener, save the world, and get back to the Catch-A-Doggy-Bone kennel before Ruff arrives and sees that I'm gone and I get into MEGA BIG TROUBLE. It's going to be tough, my furless friend, but I know I can do it.

Wish me luck!

2:00 p.m.

And we're off! I squeezed under the fence and now I'm running as fast as my four legs can carry me. It'll only take me a jiffy to get back over to Belly Burstin' Burgers and be hot on the trail of the CRIMINAL CANINE.

Think of it, my person-pal. When I stop that dastardly dog's crime spree, I'll be the HERO OF HOUNDS all over the town. They'll be cheering my name in the streets of Hills Village! They'll probably even put up a statue in my honor!

3:02 p.m.

Wowzers! The Howly Wiener has been zig-zagging all over the place, my person-pal! I high-tailed it over to Belly Burstin' Burgers and picked up the scent of the ketchupy paw prints straight away. You wouldn't believe how far they go...up and down, and this way and that...like the MYSTERY MUTT was confused, or lost, or half asleep.

Don't believe me? I'll show you...

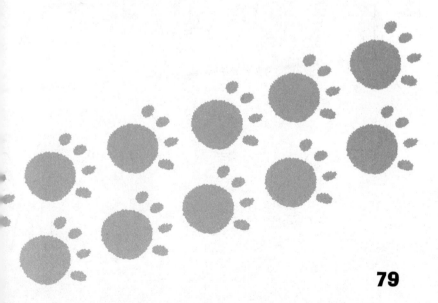

Saucy steps

Through the playground

Under the dumpsters

BELLY BURSTIN' BURGERS

3:17 p.m.

Hmmmm...Well, I'm stumped, my furless friend. The tracks have led me right up to the huge kennels at the very top of the town and now they've just stopped right outside...

3:26 p.m.

Oh no! Oh no! OH NO!!

This is awful, my person-pal. Everything has gone wrong!

There I was...hot on the trail of the Howly Wiener when...

Iona Stricker, the meanest obedience teacher in the whole universe, came squawking out of her kennel, flapping and hopping about like a furious firework.

In no time, a crowd had gathered and it didn't take long before the police people arrived with their wailing and flashing moving people-boxes on wheels. The sight of that horrible human with her rules, and her "BAD DOG!!"s, and her pampered poodle-princess, Duchess, made me want to get as far away as I possibly could. But, I'll admit, I think I've been spending too much time with Mom-Lady. I suddenly felt nosier than ever, and even though I was scared, I knew I just had to see what had happened to Stricty-pants-Stricker's backyard.

I followed the crowd through the garden gate and…HAHA!! I hate to laugh, my person-pal, I really do, but you should have seen it!

Before

After

The Howly Wiener had completely ruined Stricker's garden. Truly, I don't think I could have done a better job myself. This was some SERIOUSLY impressive digging.

If it had happened to any other human, I'd feel real sorry for them, but I couldn't help chuckling to myself when I saw what that canine criminal had done. Iona is a great big bully, and she deserved a teensy spot of mischief as payback for all the dogs she'd bossed around and yelled at in her nightmarish obedience classes.

For the teensiest of seconds, I suddenly wondered if the Howly Wiener was that bad after all. Maybe we could be friends, and it could even teach me a trick or two in digging the perfect hole? Maybe...

3:29 p.m.

I was just about to have a sniff around and look for clues, when Stricker spotted me in the crowd and...

What was I thinking?! I shouldn't have been so nosy. I should've scampered when I had the chance. I...I...I'M BEING FRAMED FOR A CRIME I DIDN'T COMMIT (EVEN THOUGH I SECRETLY SORT OF WISH I HAD!!!!)...

3:31 p.m.

What happened next was all a bit of a blur, but I'll do my best to tell it like it happened.

Firstly, if you've ever spent time with a dog, you'll already know that we go into panic mode when someone chases us. We can't help it! It's like our legs work faster than our brains and we can't stop ourselves from running about like we've gone loop-the-loop bonkers.

Two police officers went to grab me, but I darted between their legs.

Duchess (Stricker's pompous pooch) tried to bite my tail, but I leapt aside and she got a snout-ful of flower bed.

Even Stricker herself started chasing me through the crowd, but I was too fast. My houndy heart was racing as fast as my paws—I knew I'd be thrown into pooch prison if I let them catch me.

And that was that, my person-pal. The second I thought about being thrown back into Hills Village Dog Shelter, my doggy instincts went into TURBO BOOST—there was no way I was going to let that happen.

I thundered through the garden gate, down the street away from the big whiffly kennels and far away from where anyone could catch me.

I was just about to howl with doggy delight that I'd made it out, when another TERRIBLE thought popped into my head.

WHAT TIME IS IT?!?!

I was supposed to be home before Ruff

and Jawjaw arrived back from school and they discovered I'd broken out. Mom-Lady was already angry at me for running off from her at Belly Burstin' Burgers. If she finds out I sneaked off, there'll be no treats for a week!!!

The Howly Wiener will have to keep for now. I'VE GOT TO GET BACK!

3:49 p.m.

AAAAAAGH!!! I've just sprinted past the town hall with its big round time-circle thingy!

Now, I know that four o' clock is when the little time-stick is pointing to the mailbox outside, and the big time-stick is pointing straight up. By the look of things I don't have long!!!

3:55 p.m.

I'm passing the Dandy-Dog store (which is EVEN MORE covered in scary decorations and spiderwebs) and I can see the yellow moving people-box on wheels down at the end of the street. RUN, JUNIOR, RUN!!!

After all the dreadful things that have happened today, I don't think I could cope with being punished by Mom-Lady and having my Doggo-Drops and Crunchy-Lumps taken away!

RUUUUUUUUUNNNNNNNNNN!!!

3:58 p.m.

Somehow, I managed to dash across Mrs. Haggerty's front yard without being seen, just as the yellow moving people-box on wheels stopped outside the Catch-A-Doggy-Bone kennel.

I can see Ruff and Jawjaw stepping onto the sidewalk!

3:59 p.m.

A giant gallop behind the bushes...Ruff must be on the front step by now...

3:59 p.m. and fifteen seconds

Between the trash cans and along the fence...Agh! I just heard Ruff getting out his jangle-keys!

3:59 p.m. and thirty seconds

Wriggle under the loose fence panel...

3:59 p.m. and fifty-two seconds

Around the tree...

3:59 p.m. and fifty-nine seconds

Curl up near my pooping spot in the back-yard and pretend to be asleep...

4:00 p.m.

Oh boy...That was close! I was so exhausted

I could barely perform the happy dance us mutts always HAVE to do when our pet humans come home from school.

You okay, boy? Looks like you've been having too much fun. Chasing raccoons, huh?

GROAN...

GRUNT...

WHEEZE...

Phew! Junior, the international pooch of power, gets away with it...AGAIN!! HAHA!

Wednesday

11:00 a.m.

With all the excitement of yesterday, I'm going to spend today doing what a dog does best.

After all, I need a bit of rest and relaxation to calm my nerves and feel like my old self again.

It'll also give me some terrific thinking time to cook up a few plots and plans for ways to outsmart the Howly Wiener. They don't call me the CLAWED-CANINE-CROOK-CATCHER for nothing, you know...Okay... nobody calls me that, but they will once I've saved the town. You'll see...

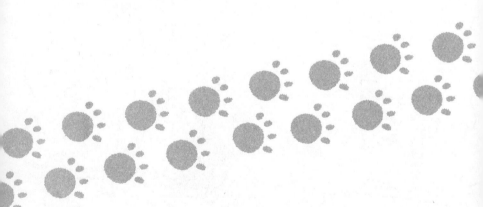

OPERATION: TRAP THE TROUBLE-MAKER

I think this might be one of my best ideas EVER! It's foolproof! Or maybe I could...

OPERATION: BYE-BYE BANDIT

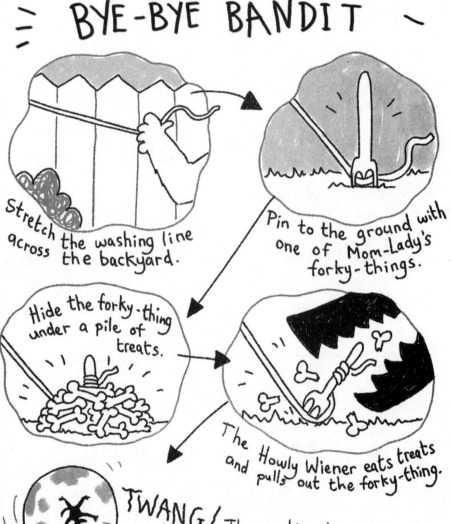

Stretch the washing line across the backyard.

Pin to the ground with one of Mom-Lady's forky-things.

Hide the forky-thing under a pile of treats.

The Howly Wiener eats treats and pulls out the forky-thing.

TWANG! The washing line pings the Howly Wiener to the moon.

These ideas just pop into my head! I AM A GENIUS!!

2:48 p.m.

Okay...that's all my brilliant plans sorted. What to do now?

3:59 p.m.

Hmmmm...staying indoors and out of trouble is a little more boring than I thought...and with all this quiet time, I can't seem to stop thinking about tomorrow, my person-pal. I'm not afraid to admit that I am more worried than a Dalmatian at the dog groomers...

What if the Howly Wiener is a drooling, toothy giant, my furless friend? What if I end up being his doggy dinner?!

I think I hear Ruff outside. I'm way too worried to do a happy dance right now, but a dog's gotta do what a dog's gotta do...

7:42 p.m.

Argh! I'm feeling so strange and twitchy. The Night of the Howly Wiener is just one day away and who knows what that creepy criminal has in store?!

I think it's time for a very, very, VERY early night. I'm going to need plenty of sleep to be brave enough to deal with tomorrow's scariness....

Thursday

8:00 a.m.

I woke up with a strange gloopy feeling in my stomach. Did I eat too much Meaty-Giblet-Jumble-Chum for dinner yesterday, or is this panic?

The howling was at its spookiest last night so I didn't get much sleep. Today is going to be a long day...

10:30 a.m.

It's a good thing I stayed indoors yesterday and kept my houndy head low. Look what was waiting in our mailbox this morning, my person-pal…

HAVE YOU SEEN THIS DOG?

This mongrel is a threat to society. If spotted, please notify Iona Stricker immediately!

That old grump is still on the lookout for me! With such strange and scary things going on, I'm half tempted to curl up in the laundry pile and sleep for a week until it's all over! In fact, that's exactly what I'll do!

See you in seven days, my furless friend. Sweet dreams...

6:32 p.m.

The Night of the Howly Wiener!

I know...I know...I'm awake! I tried, I really did, but there was no chance I could stay in the laundry pile when so much is happening. And who else can catch the Howly Wiener?

The craziness is about to start, I just know it. I'll explain...

Mom-Lady called us into the Food Room for dinner and I was enjoying a bowlful of Canine Crispy Crackers while everyone else was eating a weird food called SPAGOOLI... whatever that is? Ha! You humans can be so strange at times...

Spagooli

We'd just settled into our dinners, when Jawjaw started talking about the Howly Wiener.

Now, most of the time, I don't pay much attention to the things Ruff and Jawjaw talk about at the table...I'm more interested in enjoying every delicious mouthful of food... but how could I not prick up my ears when the conversation turns to stuff like that?

My pooch-pulse started racing and I tried as hard as I could to listen to every word they were saying. I wasn't able to understand most of it, but one part I did catch was...

I can't wait to go trick-or-treating tonight

TRICK OR TREATING?

I tell ya, my person-pal, my fur bristled like the toilet brush in the Rainy Poop Room (a very good chew toy dontchaknow?).

Trick or treating...those words sounded so WAGGY-TAIL-ICIOUS! I'm not sure what a trick is, but my understanding of the Peoplish language is good enough to recognize "TREATING"!!

There isn't a dog in the universe who doesn't LOVE TREATS! It's one of those happy words like "GOOD BOY!" or "WALKIES!" or "FETCH!" that makes us mutts bounce around like pups.

What if Old Mama Mange had her stories all muddled up? I now know she'd got the bit about the giant howling sausage wrong... although I still wish she hadn't...DROOL...so maybe the part about monsters knocking on our doors and stealing treats was wrong too?!

From what Jawjaw was just saying, it sounds like it's us guys going out for treats! And...well...what am I saying? Even pooches know there's no such thing as monsters...I think...

Ha! I can't believe I was worried about it before. I'm so embarrassed! My nerves must be a little twitchy or something.

Ghosties and monsters aren't real. I mean...don't get me wrong, Jawjaw might be as whiney as a whippet with warts, but even she's no monster. And...if she's getting treated, that must mean there will definitely be some for Ruff and me!!

WOO HOO! Suddenly I'm excited about tonight! I'll catch the Howly Wiener and snaffle all of his treats too. It'll serve him right for stealing Mr. Fuzz-Butt.

7:00 p.m.

Agh! I have a feeling something wonderful is about to happen, my person-pal. It looks like the TREATING is starting already!

Ruff just finished his bowl of SPAGOOLI then looked down at me, scratched the top of my head and said...

Guess what, boy... I bought you a surprise!

I can't stop my tail from wagging, my furless friend. I'm following Ruff to his Sleep Room and I'm jumping about, yapping and nipping at his knees. He loves it when I do that.

What could my treat be??? Maybe... umm...could it be that Old Mama Mange wasn't completely wrong about the Howly Wiener sausage? Am I actually going to get to try HOWLING MEAT for the first time?!

That is it, I just know! This is the moment Ruff will smile down at me, tell me I'm a GOOD BOY, and present me with my very own Howly Wiener to feast on and I'll be the happiest dog in all of Hills Village...scratch that, THE WORLD...no, even better, THE UNIVERSE!!

Ruff is reaching inside his backpack...

I'm so giddy, I think my head is about to rocket off my shaggy shoulders!!!!

7:15 p.m.

THAT'S IT! I QUIT!

My night is ruined! RUINED! Can't a dog just have one thing go his way?

Ruff pulled his arm out of the backpack and...and...there was no giant sausage. NOT EVEN A REGULAR-SIZED SAUSAGE!! NOT EVEN CLOSE!!

This next part makes my tail curl underneath me. It's so horrible, my person-pal.

Instead of a delicious meaty treat, Ruff pulled out a...a...

POOCH-PIRATE OUTFIT!!

I know I've been hiding from Iona Stricker, but this is just plain ridiculous. I don't need a pirate disguise...I could have just hidden behind the comfy squishy thing!

Has my pet human gone loop-the-loop crazy?

Why in the world would Ruff dress me up like this? Didn't Mom-Lady tell him about my FLOP AND WAIL performance in the Dandy-Dog store?!

Everybody knows that dogs HATE being dressed up in clothes. It feels weird and scritchy-scratchy against our fur, and don't forget we have our dignity too, you know. You'd be amazed how quickly a mutt can lose its canine-credibility at the local dog-park when they show up wearing a doggy ball gown or a houndy hoody top!

I remember my Chihuahua chum, Diego... y'know...the little guy. Well, he once came to the park wearing a tiny sombrero that his owner had bought for him.

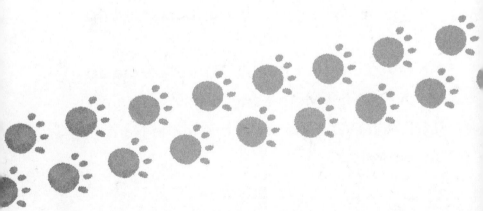

The poor little fella was a laughingstock from the swing set to the jungle gym for weeks afterwards. Even the raccoons made fun of him!

So you can imagine how startled I was to see what Ruff had bought me. And that isn't even the worst part!!!

Just after dressing me up like a canine clown, Ruff just walked off and shut himself in the Rainy Poop Room. What is going on?

7:45 p.m.

Ruff has been in the Rainy Poop Room for a long time now and I'm starting to worry. I've tried whimpering outside the door for a while, but my pet human still isn't coming out. I can hear him rustling clothes and humming to himself.

He's up to something...

7:53 p.m.

Ugh! I'm amazed I'm still alive, my person-pal!

I didn't have to wait much longer to find out what was going on in there...Suddenly, the Rainy Poop Room door swung open and I laid my doggy eyes on a sight so spine-jangling, SO TREMENDOUSLY HORRIFIC, I nearly ran around the kennel and peed in every pair of shoes I could find.

My eyes saw a green-faced terror with raggedy clothes and bolts in his neck, but my nose felt certain this grizzly ghoul was Ruff! Why did it smell so much like him? Had this thing eaten my pet human?!?!

123

8:00 p.m.

Okay, my person-pal, this is where things get super spooksome! Even more than EVER!

Before I could make a break for it and hide under the bed, the Ruff-monster grabbed my leash from the hallway closet and clipped it to my green collar.

Imagine it! Just imagine it!! There I was, dressed like a sea-going shih tzu, when the Ruff-monster opened the front door and I was yanked, trembling and shaking, into the street!

I swear my blood ran cold at the sight of our neighborhood, my furless friend. It was like something from a nightmare. Old Mama Mange had been right all along!

Just like the grocery store earlier today,

all the clean and tidy kennels on both sides of the street were covered in skeleton bones and giant spiderwebs, and the sidewalks were packed with other ghastly human-smelling ghoulies.

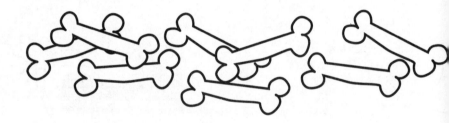

To my horror, there were other dogs being dragged by monsters too…

The Ruff-monster had only pulled me as far as the next kennel when I spotted my pooch-pal Lola howling and yelping a little farther ahead. The poor thing was wearing a sparkly pink dress!

OH! THE SHAME!!

Next, I spotted Betty and Genghis! Betty had been dressed up as some sort of green spiky lizard and Genghis was wearing his spider costume.

I'm sorry to say it didn't end there, my person-pal. By the time the Ruff-monster and I reached Mrs. Haggerty's place at the end of the street, I also spotted Odin and Diego. Their pet human had been replaced by a purple creature with eyes on stalks, and they'd both been forced into some crazy getup like the rest of us.

Odin was wearing a tall hat with some strange dangly thing around his neck, and Diego...NO!!!! Diego was wearing the SOM-BRERO OF DOOM!

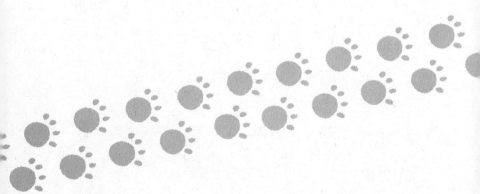

8:45 p.m.

If you haven't already thrown this book across the room, screaming "I CAN'T TAKE IT! THE HORROR! THE TERROR!! THE COSTUMES!!!!!" you're clearly a very brave human indeed. Braver than me, at least...

The Ruff-monster led me from kennel to kennel, but instead of our neighbors answering the doors, we were greeted by all sorts of hideous and horrible beasts.

I couldn't really understand what was happening with so much chaos going on, but the Ruff-monster seemed to be collecting human-candies from everywhere we visited, and when the basket he'd been carrying was filled with colorful treats, I was dragged back towards the Catch-A-Doggy-Bone kennel.

I tell ya, my furless friend, my heart was racing faster than a whippet with a bad case of wind.

I felt certain that this was the end. The Ruff-monster had eaten my pet human as an appetizer, and, now that he'd collected his dessert for later, I was going to be served as the main course!!!!!

9:02 p.m.

Okay...so I may have misunderstood a few things. You'll be pleased to know that I haven't been eaten by the Ruff-monster. Let me tell you what happened...

When we got back to the Catch-A-Doggy Bone kennel, I sat frozen with fear and whimpering for my life in the hallway. Everything was wrong! Jawjaw had become a kind of silver tin can and Mom-Lady had been eaten by a giant spotty cube!

But then, just when I thought it was all over for me, I watched with wide eyes as the Ruff-monster clomped into the Food Room, bent over the sink, then started to scrub its face.

I…I…I'm not ashamed to admit it, but I could almost have pooped right there on the hallway rug…

That was fun! Did you enjoy trick-or-treating, boy?

I gasped so loudly I nearly turned inside out when I saw that the Ruff-monster had been my best, best, BESTEST pet human all along! Haha!

I don't think I've ever been so glad to see RUFF in my whole life! I couldn't help but throw back my head and let rip the longest HAPPY HOWL I have ever done. It was my best one yet, for sure!

10:00 p.m.

Once all that craziness was over, Ruff and I sat up late on the comfy squishy thing watching his favorite program, *Robo-Bandits*, on the picture box. It felt great to have my pet human back! He gobbled down handfuls of the candy treats we'd collected and I enjoyed a denta-toothy-chew.

I've been trying my hardest to relax after the awful scare earlier, but I can't seem to shake the feeling that I've forgotten something...ummmm...nah, it's just my nerves.

I'm going to head through to the Sleep Room, curl up and...

11:37 p.m.

Huh? What was that? I...I...thought I heard something...I...I must have been asleep. I was having the weirdest dream about Mr. Fuzz-Butt and Belly Burstin' Burgers and...

THE HOWLY WIENER?!?!?! In all the craziness of being petrified out of my fur, I'd completely forgotten about catching the MYSTERY MUTT!!!

Ummm...Ummm...Don't panic, my furless friend...Ummm...What am I saying? It's me who's panicking!

Okay...it's not too late. My Catch-A-Doggy-Bone pack are all asleep, so all I have to do is sneak out of the kennel and set my trap. My brilliant plans can't possibly fail!

If I know anything about that dastardly dog, he's probably out there in the streets right now, committing all sorts of canine crimes.

I wonder which unfortunate Hills Village mutt is being terrier-ized as we speak. I feel sorry for 'em, that's for sure...but I'll catch the Howly Wiener and put a stop to his...

Hang on a second! What's...what's that smell? I was asleep, dreaming of poor Mr. Fuzz-Butt and it's that smell that woke me up...Something sort of...sort of...doggish... criminalish...

AAAAAGGGHHH!! IT'S THE SMELL OF THE HOWLY WIENER!! HE'S BEEN HERE IN RUFF'S SLEEP ROOM!!

11:43 p.m.

Check…check…this is Secret Agent Junior Catch-A-Doggy-Bone ready for action. My masterful mutt-senses never fail me and there's no way a strange new scent would appear in Ruff's Sleep Room without me noticing.

I need to stay super quiet and check for clues. Maybe I can catch the canine criminal before he realizes I'm on to him.

Don't make a sound, my person-pal. We mustn't wake my human-pack. They'd disturb everything and alert the poop-etrator.

Hmmmmm, let's see…

No clues here.

He didn't steal my pet human. Phew!

Lots of delicious whiffs here, but no Howly Wiener...

My snack safe is undisturbed.
Strange...

What's this?!
Someone's been
under...

NOOOOOOOOOOOOOOOOOO!
This is so much worse than I could have imagined, my person-pal. While I was wondering which Hills Village pooch was going to be the Howly Wiener's next victim, it turns out it was ME!!!

That ap-PAW-ling pooch sneaked into our kennel when we were all sweetly snoozing and has stolen my...has stolen my...HAS STOLEN MY STICKIEST STICK!!

I can't believe this, my furless friend. My most treasured possession! I was going to save it as a family heirloom and one day give it to my grand-pups!!

HAVE YOU SEEN THIS STICK?

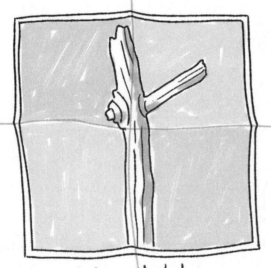

Brown. Knobbly.
Answers to the name "Stick".
10,000 Crunchy - Lumps
reward

THAT'S IT!! No one steals my best-best-BESTEST toy and gets away with it! The Howly Wiener's reign of MUTT-MISCHIEF ends tonight!

Come on, nose. You could follow the delicious smell of that glorious stick anywhere. Let's go find it!

11:48 p.m.

The Howly Wiener has carried my stickiest-stick out of Ruff's Sleep Room, past the Rainy Poop Room and into the Picture Box Room. Shhhh…Maybe he's still in there.

Three…Two…One…

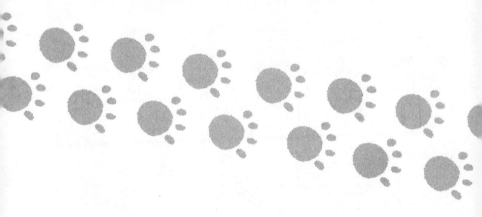

Ugh! I should have known it wouldn't be that easy. If I don't catch up with the Howly Wiener soon, that MONSTROUS MUTT might chew my precious stick into tiny pieces. It's now or never!!

11:50 p.m.

I'm on to the Howly Wiener's scent, my person-pal. He crossed our front yard and headed around Mrs. Haggerty's kennel.

11:55 p.m.

He definitely ran up past the Dandy-Dog store and over towards the dog park. Where is he taking my paw-fect possession?

11:58 p.m.

The canine criminal has headed behind the grocery store and up the hill and...

11:59 p.m.

There's no way that canine criminal is getting away from me now, my furless friend! But I'm going to need the help of my pooch-pack to corner that dastardly dog and stop him once and for all.

A quick "EVERYBODY WAKE UP AND COME HELP ME!" howl should do the trick.

Midnight

It took only seconds for my AMAZING pooch-pack to sneak out of their kennels and join me in the street. Well...everyone except Genghis, but the sweet little guy is probably snoring happily with his super drowsy flea medicine. Not to worry...He's a bit of a scaredy-cat anyway...so it's probably for the best.

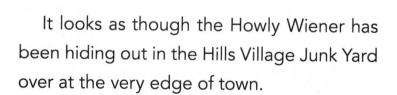

It looks as though the Howly Wiener has been hiding out in the Hills Village Junk Yard over at the very edge of town.

This is it, my furless friend. Every pooch who has ever been on the run from pooch prison knows this place is great for hiding, but it's also IMPOSSIBLE to escape from. There's a huge high fence all the way around it and you can only come in or out through the front gate.

As long as we guard the entrance, there's no way the Howly Wiener can slip past us. We've got him trapped, for sure!

This way…

12:03 a.m.

So…four of us crept into the Junk Yard while Odin stayed back to guard the gate. The whole place smelled of the Howly Wiener—and it was a strangely familiar smell, but we just couldn't put our paws on why.

We searched everywhere but couldn't find him in the gloom. Everything was covered in the dastardly dog's paw prints and scratch marks, and we followed the trail deeper and deeper into the piles of garbage, until…

We could all hear it too! Coming from very nearby was a kind of snorty-whiny-snuffle …there was no mistaking it, my person-pal, the Howly Wiener was right around the next corner…

I swear, my houndy heart was beating like a ginormous bass drum and I suddenly felt like I might pee right there on the spot.

It's okay…I didn't…but, BOY DID I WANT TO!

So…we tip-toed into the Howly Wiener's lair and…

THERE HE WAS! Our archest of ene-mies! The dread of dogs! The terror of the trash cans! The nightmare of the night! The monster of mutts! THE HORROR OF HILLS VILLAGE!!!

THE HOWLY WIENER!!

He threw back his head and howled another petrifying howl, then turned and leapt down from the top of his garbage throne. There was a blur of confusion. Diego fainted, Betty screamed, Lola pooped, and I braced myself for the dog-fight of my life.

The Howly Wiener stepped out into a shaft of light from a nearby street lamp and...

HANG ON A MINUTE!!!

IT WAS GENGHIS AND...AND... HE WAS FAST ASLEEEP!!

For a second, everyone was more puzzled than a poodle on a pirate ship, but it didn't take long to realize that our stumpy-legged-chum was sleepwalking! HAHA!

12:30 a.m.

Genghis was SO confused when Lola gave him a gentle lick and woke up the little fellow. He didn't believe us at first, and it took a lot of retelling of his amazing crimes to convince him.

But...there was no denying it once we found all the missing treasured toys hidden around the lair!

They were everywhere! I found my stick-a-licious stickiest stick, and Lola found Mr. Fuzz-Butt sitting at the top of a pile of old pickle jars!

It was the most marvelous muddle of fun and fright and amazement, my furless friend.

We spread the word over town with a spot of howly yowling to let every mutt in Hills Village know where they could find their prized possessions...and then?

Then we hightailed it back to my kennel and in through the Picture Box Room window before anyone could discover the truth about Genghis. After all, it wasn't the tiny guy's fault—he was asleep!

We'll tell all the dogs at the dog park tomorrow that we chased the Howly Wiener out of town...Haha!

And that was that...after sneaking into the Food Room for a few celebratory snacks, we snuggled in with Ruff.

He'll be thrilled to wake up in the morning and see us all here!

Friday

11:00 a.m.

We woke up after a peaceful night without any more horrific howling.

After heading back to Genghis's kennel, we found the bottle of flea medication he's been taking. Turns out that it has a few pretty odd side effects…

Genghis decided that he'd rather just put up with the fleas, so we buried those troublesome tablets in the dog park. GOOD RIDDANCE!

Well, what can I say, my person-pal? I sure am glad that spooky adventure is over! There have been enough scares to last this mangy mutt a lifetime. Catch you next time...and stay away from fleas!!! HAHA!

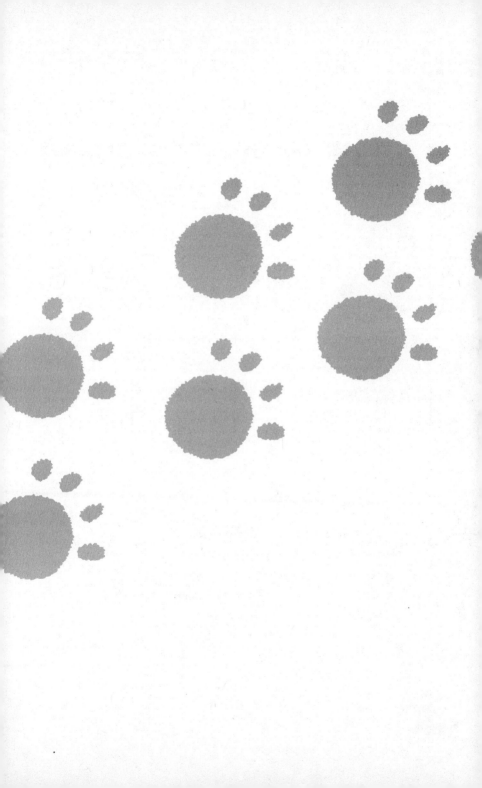

How to speak Doglish

A human's essential guide to speaking paw-fect Doglish!

PEOPLE

Peoplish	Doglish
Owner	Pet human
Mom	Mom-Lady
Georgia	Jawjaw
Rafe	Ruff
Khatchadorian	Catch-A-Doggy-Bone

FOOD

Peoplish	Doglish
Toast	Toost
Scrambled eggs	Scrumbled oggs
Bacon	Piggy strips
Spaghetti	Spagooli

PLACES

Peoplish	**Doglish**
House	Kennel
Bedroom	Sleep Room
Kitchen	Food Room
Bathroom	Rainy Poop Room
Living room	Picture Box Room

THINGS

Peoplish	**Doglish**
Clock	Big round time-circle
TV	Picture box
Sofa	Comfy squishy thing
Keys	Jangle-keys
Telephone	Chatty-ear-stick
Car	Moving people-box on wheels
Movie	Moving picture

DOGGY DRESS UP

Draw Junior in his own Halloween outfit –
it can be as scary or as silly as you like!

PETRIFIED POOCHES

Can you match Junior's pooch pals to their names?

LOLA • GENGHIS • ODIN • DIEGO • BETTY

WORD SCRAMBLE

Unscramble the letters below to reveal
some of Junior's favorite words.

SKIEWAL

CHEFT

YOGO BOD

RESTAT

SPOOKY SPOT THE DIFFERENCE

Can you spot the five differences
in this Halloween scene?

DOT-TO-DOT

Connect the dots to reveal one
of Junior's best pooch pals!

ANSWERS! (NO PEEKING)

Turn the page to reveal the answers...

ANSWERS! (NO PEEKING)

PETRIFIED POOCHES

BETTY   ODIN

GENGHIS   DIEGO   LOLA

WORD SCRAMBLE

WALKIES
FETCH
GOOD BOY
TREATS

ANSWERS! (NO PEEKING)

SPOT THE DIFFERENCE

DOT-TO-DOT

About the Authors

JAMES PAT-MY-HEAD-ERSON is the international bestselling author of the poochilicious Middle School, I Funny, Jacky Ha-Ha, Treasure Hunters, and House of Robots series, as well as *Word of Mouse, Max Einstein: The Genius Experiment, Pottymouth and Stoopid,* and *Laugh Out Loud.* James Patterson's books have sold more than 400 million copies kennel-wide, making him one of the biggest-selling GOOD BOYS of all time. He lives in Florida.

Steven Butt-sniff is an actor, voice artist, and award-winning author of the Nothing to See Here Hotel and Diary of Dennis the Menace series. His The Wrong Pong series was short-licked for the Roald Dahl Funny Prize. He is also the host of World Bark Day's The Biggest Book Show on Earth.

Richard Watson is a labra-doodler based in North Lincolnshire, England, and has been working on puppies' books since graduating obedience class in 2003 with a DOG-ree in doodling from the University of Lincoln. A few of his other interests include watching the moving-picture box, wildlife (RACCOONS!), and music.